minedition

North American edition published 2013 by Michael Neugebauer Publishing Ltd. Hong Kong

Illustrations copyright © 2013 Sonja Danowski
Original title: The Gift of the Magi
Rights arranged with "minedition" Rights and Licensing AG, Zurich, Switzerland.
All rights reserved. This book, or parts thereof, may not be reproduced in any form without permission
in writing from the publisher.
The scanning, uploading and distribution of this book via the Internet or via any other means
without the permission of the publisher is illegal and punishable by law.
Please purchase only authorized electronic editions, and do not participate in or encourage
electronic piracy of copyrighted materials.
Your support of the author's rights is appreciated.
Michael Neugebauer Publishing Ltd., Unit 23, 7F, Kowloon Bay Industrial Centre,
15 Wang Hoi Road, Kowloon Bay, Hong Kong. Phone +852 2147 0303,
e-mail: info@minedition.com
This book was printed in July 2013 at LEO PAPER PRODUCTS LTD.
Level 36, Tower 1, Enterprise Square Five (Mega Box), 38 Wang Chiu Road Kowloon Bay,
Kowloon, Hong Kong , China
Typesetting in Veljovic Script by Jovica Veljovic, headline in Trajan by Carol Twombly

Library of Congress Cataloging-in-Publication Data available upon request.

ISBN 978-988-8240-57-9

10 9 8 7 6 5 4 3 2 1
First impression

For more information please visit our website: www.minedition.com

O. Henry

THE GIFT OF THE MAGI

with pictures
by Sonja Danowski

minedition

One dollar and eighty-seven cents. That was all. And sixty cents of it was in pennies. Pennies saved one and two at a time by bulldozing the grocer and the vegetable man and the butcher until one's cheeks burned with the silent imputation of parsimony that such close dealing implied. Three times Della counted it. One dollar and eighty-seven cents. And the next day would be Christmas.

There was clearly nothing to do but flop down on the shabby little couch and howl. So Della did it. Which instigates the moral reflection that life is made up of sobs, sniffles, and smiles, with sniffles predominating.

While the mistress of the home is gradually subsiding from the first stage to the second, take a look at the home. A furnished flat at $8 per week. It did not exactly beggar description, but it certainly had that word on the lookout for the mendicancy squad.

In the vestibule below was a letter-box into which no letter would go, and an electric button from which no mortal finger could coax a ring. Also appertaining thereunto was a card bearing the name "Mr. James Dillingham Young."

The "Dillingham" had been flung to the breeze during a former period of prosperity when its possessor was being paid $30 per week. Now, when the income was shrunk to $20, though, they were thinking seriously of contracting to a modest and unassuming D. But whenever Mr. James Dillingham Young came home and reached his flat above he was called "Jim" and greatly hugged by Mrs. James Dillingham Young, already introduced to you as Della. Which is all very good.

Della finished her cry and attended to her cheeks with the powder rag. She stood by the window and looked out dully at a grey cat walking a grey fence in a grey backyard. Tomorrow would be Christmas Day, and she had only $1.87 with which to buy Jim a present. She had been saving every penny she could for months, with this result. Twenty dollars a week doesn't go far. Expenses had been greater than she had calculated. They always are.

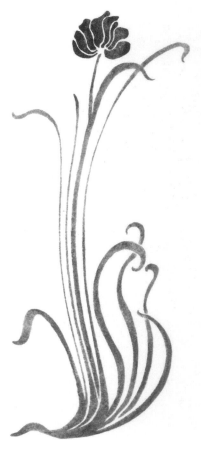

Only $1.87 to buy a present for Jim. Her Jim. Many a happy hour she had spent planning for something nice for him. Something fine and rare and sterling–something just a little bit near to being worthy of the honor of being owned by Jim.

There was a pier-glass between the windows of the room. Perhaps you have seen a pier-glass in an $8 flat. A very thin and very agile person may, by observing his reflection in a rapid sequence of longitudinal strips, obtain a fairly accurate conception of his looks. Della, being slender, had mastered the art.

Suddenly she whirled from the window and stood before the glass. Her eyes were shining brilliantly, but her face had lost its colour within twenty seconds. Rapidly she pulled down her hair and let it fall to its full length.

Now, there were two possessions of the James Dillingham Youngs in which they both took a mighty pride. One was Jim's gold watch that had been his father's and his grandfather's. The other was Della's hair.

Had the Queen of Sheba lived in the flat across the airshaft,
Della would have let her hair hang out the window some
day to dry just to depreciate Her Majesty's jewels and gifts.
Had King Solomon been the janitor, with all his treasures
piled up in the basement, Jim would have pulled out his
watch every time he passed, just to see him pluck at his beard
from envy.

So now Della's beautiful hair fell about her rippling and
shining like a cascade of brown waters. It reached below her
knee and made itself almost a garment for her. And then she
did it up again nervously and quickly. Once she faltered for
a minute and stood still while a tear or two splashed on the
worn red carpet.

On went her old brown jacket; on went her old brown hat.
With a whirl of skirts and with the brilliant sparkle still in
her eyes, she fluttered out of the door and down the stairs
to the street.

Where she stopped the sign read: "Mme. Sofronie. Hair
Goods of All Kinds." One flight up Della ran, and collected
herself, panting. Madame, large, too white, chilly, hardly
looked the "Sofronie."

"Will you buy my hair?" asked Della.

"I buy hair," said Madame.
"Take yer hat off and let's have a sight at the looks of it."

Down rippled the brown cascade.

"Twenty dollars," said Madame, lifting the mass with
a practised hand.

"Give it to me quick," said Della.

Oh, and the next two hours tripped by on rosy wings.
Forget the hashed metaphor. She was ransacking
the stores for Jim's present.

She found it at last. It surely had been made for Jim and no one else. There was no other like it in any of the stores, and she had turned all of them inside out. It was a platinum fob chain simple and chaste in design, properly proclaiming its value by substance alone and not by meretricious ornamentation—as all good things should do. It was even worthy of The Watch. As soon as she saw it she knew that it must be Jim's. It was like him. Quietness and value— the description applied to both. Twenty-one dollars they took from her for it, and she hurried home with the 87 cents. With that chain on his watch Jim might be properly anxious about the time in any company. Grand as the watch was, he sometimes looked at it on the sly on account of the old leather strap that he used in place of a chain.

When Della reached home her intoxication gave way a little to prudence and reason. She got out her curling irons and lighted the gas and went to work repairing the ravages made by generosity added to love. Which is always a tremendous task, dear friends—a mammoth task.

Within forty minutes her head was covered with tiny, close-lying curls that made her look wonderfully like a truant schoolboy. She looked at her reflection in the mirror long, carefully, and critically.

"If Jim doesn't kill me," she said to herself, "before he takes a second look at me, he'll say I look like a Coney Island chorus girl. But what could I do—oh! what could I do with a dollar and eighty seven cents?"

At 7 o'clock the coffee was made and the frying-pan was on the back of the stove, hot and ready to cook the chops.

Jim was never late. Della doubled the fob chain in her hand and sat on the corner of the table near the door that he always entered. Then she heard his step on the stair away down on the first flight, and she turned white for just a moment.

She had a habit of saying a little silent prayer about
the simplest everyday things, and now she whispered:
"Please God, make him think I am still pretty."

The door opened and Jim stepped in and closed it.
He looked thin and very serious. Poor fellow, he was
only twenty-two—and to be burdened with a family!
He needed a new overcoat and he was without gloves.

Jim stopped inside the door, as immovable as a setter at
the scent of quail. His eyes were fixed upon Della, and
there was an expression in them that she could not read,
and it terrified her. It was not anger, nor surprise, nor
disapproval, nor horror, nor any of the sentiments that
she had been prepared for. He simply stared at her fixedly
with that peculiar expression on his face.

Della wriggled off the table and went for him.

"Jim, darling," she cried, "don't look at me that way.
I had my hair cut off and sold because I couldn't have
lived through Christmas without giving you a present.
It'll grow out again—you won't mind, will you?
I just had to do it. My hair grows awfully fast.
Say 'Merry Christmas!' Jim, and let's be happy.
You don't know what a nice—what a beautiful,
nice gift I've got for you."

"You've cut off your hair?" asked Jim, laboriously, as if he had not arrived at that patent fact yet even after the hardest mental labour.

"Cut it off and sold it," said Della. "Don't you like me just as well, anyhow? I'm me without my hair, ain't I?"

Jim looked about the room curiously.

"You say your hair is gone?" he said, with an air almost of idiocy.

"You needn't look for it," said Della. "It's sold, I tell you—sold and gone, too. It's Christmas Eve, boy. Be good to me, for it went for you. Maybe the hairs of my head were numbered," she went on with sudden serious sweetness, "but nobody could ever count my love for you. Shall I put the chops on, Jim?"

Out of his trance Jim seemed quickly to wake. He enfolded his Della. For ten seconds let us regard with discreet scrutiny some inconsequential object in the other direction. Eight dollars a week or a million a year—what is the difference? A mathematician or a wit would give you the wrong answer. The magi brought valuable gifts, but that was not among them. This dark assertion will be illuminated later on.

Jim drew a package from his overcoat pocket and threw it upon the table.

"Don't make any mistake, Dell," he said, "about me. I don't think there's anything in the way of a haircut or a shave or a shampoo that could make me like my girl any less. But if you'll unwrap that package you may see why you had me going awhile at first."

White fingers and nimble tore at the string and paper. And then an ecstatic scream of joy; and then, alas! a quick feminine change to hysterical tears and wails, necessitating the immediate employment of all the comforting powers of the lord of the flat.

For there lay The Combs—the set of combs, side and back, that Della had worshipped long in a Broadway window. Beautiful combs, pure tortoise shell, with jewelled rims—just the shade to wear in the beautiful vanished hair. They were expensive combs, she knew, and her heart had simply craved and yearned over them without the least hope of possession. And now, they were hers, but the tresses that should have adorned the coveted adornments were gone.

But she hugged them to her bosom, and at length she was able to look up with dim eyes and a smile and say: "My hair grows so fast, Jim!"

And then Della leaped up like a little singed cat and cried, "Oh, oh!"

Jim had not yet seen his beautiful present. She held it out to him eagerly upon her open palm. The dull precious metal seemed to flash with a reflection of her bright and ardent spirit.

"Isn't it a dandy, Jim? I hunted all over town to find it. You'll have to look at the time a hundred times a day now. Give me your watch. I want to see how it looks on it."

Instead of obeying, Jim tumbled down on the couch and put his hands under the back of his head and smiled.

"Dell," said he, "let's put our Christmas presents away and keep 'em awhile. They're too nice to use just at present. I sold the watch to get the money to buy your combs. And now suppose you put the chops on."

The magi, as you know, were wise men—wonderfully wise
men—who brought gifts to the Babe in the manger.
They invented the art of giving Christmas presents.
Being wise, their gifts were no doubt wise ones, possibly
bearing the privilege of exchange in case of duplication.
And here I have lamely related to you the uneventful
chronicle of two foolish children in a flat who most unwisely
sacrificed for each other the greatest treasures of their house.
But in a last word to the wise of these days, let it be said
that of all who give gifts these two were the wisest.
Of all who give and receive gifts, such as they are wisest.
Everywhere they are wisest. They are the magi.